A chosen path lies before me,
red, white, and blue.
Unsung heroes in service...

United States Armed Forces
protecting you.

Your woobie keeps you warm
as I lace my boots before sunrise.
You are my trinket,
the treasure in my eye.

At times, I am pulled away,
near or far, over thousands of miles.
Across oceans and mountains,
my heart yearns for your smiles.

When it's time to part,
I'll give you a kiss and shed a few tears.
The plane waits silently while I whisper,
"See you later. Be brave and have no fear."

Although I am sad to go,
adventure awaits both
me and you.

I go my way and you go yours,
we'll follow our rule to try
something new.

At moments of despair, climb the winding mountain, discover the bald eagle in all of her beauty. She guards the homeland and in her fierce eyes...

You'll find peace
and the understanding of duty.

Whispering in the wind,
Old Glory you will find.
Give her a salute and remember,
no boots are left behind.

Patriotism runs deep
in those who serve,
brimming with pride, love, and humility,
for the country they deserve.

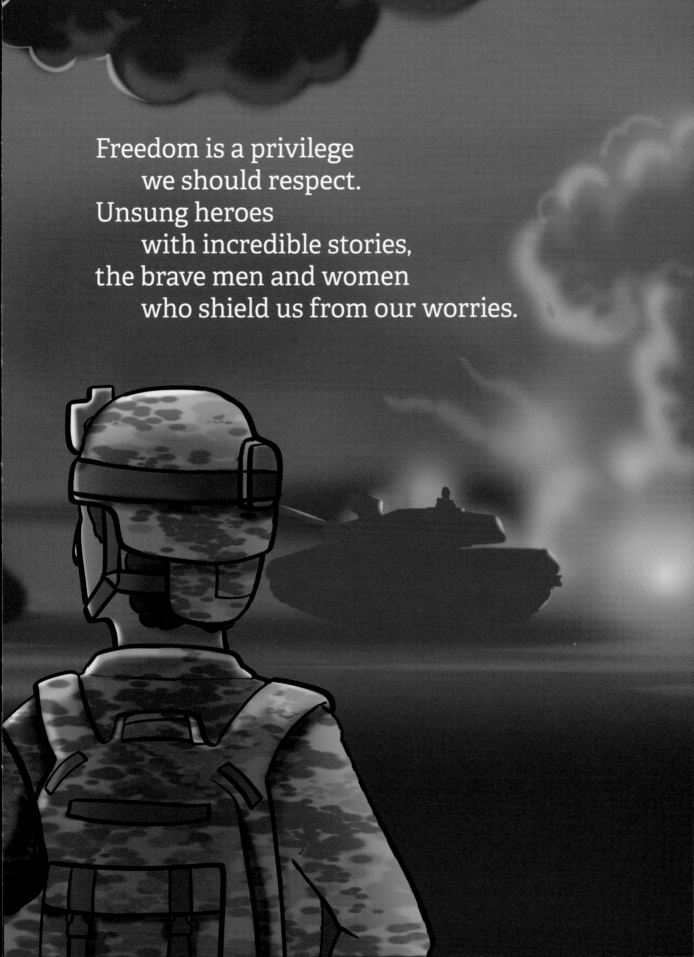

Freedom is a privilege
	we should respect.
Unsung heroes
	with incredible stories,
the brave men and women
	who shield us from our worries.

Have courage, my dear,
for I am not far.
Look up to the sky
for the Northern Star.

I wear this uniform,
I wear it for you.
My greatest honor
is seeing it through.

And upon my return,
from the day we kissed goodbye,
you will forever be...

My Unsung Hero,
my Fourth of July!

ABOUT THE AUTHOR

Maria Cordova is an Army wife, Navy brat, mom of two beautiful girls, *Military Times* contributor, member of Team Red, White, and Blue, and author of the children's book *The ABCs of the Army.*

Visit her online at
MARIACORDOVA.COM